Bantam Books in the Choose Your Own Adventure® Series
Ask your bookseller for the books you have missed.

VAMPIRE EXPRESS

By TONY KOLTZ

ILLUSTRATED BY DOUG JAMIESON

A Packard/Montgomery Book

BANTAM BOOKS
NEW YORK · TORONTO · LONDON · SYDNEY · AUCKLAND

RL 4, IL age 10 and up

VAMPIRE EXPRESS

A Bantam Book / April 1984

2nd printing .... April 1984	6th printing .... June 1985
3rd printing .... April 1984	7th printing ..... March 1986
4th printing .... April 1984	8th printing .... July 1987
5th printing .... October 1984	9th printing .... May 1988

Original conception of Edward Packard

Produced by Cloverdale Press Inc.
133 Ffith Ave., New York, N.Y. 10003

ISBN 0-553-27053-2

Published simultaneously in the United States and Canada

PRINTED IN THE UNITED STATES OF AMERICA

O   18 17 16 15 14 13 12 11

For David and Jonathan

WARNING!!!!

Do not read this book straight through from beginning to end! It contains many adventures you may have riding the *Vampire Express* and tracking down those elusive, bloodthirsty creatures of night: vampires! From time to time as you read along, you will be asked to make decisions and choices. Some of them are dangerous.!

What happens to you will be the result of your choices. *You* are responsible because *you* choose. After you make each choice, follow the instructions to see what happens to you next.

Think carefully before you make a decision. You could end up being one of the vampires' victims— or you could put an end to their fiendish attacks forever!

You're on a train in the Carpathian Mountains of Romania, on your way to visit your uncle Andrew. In all the world there is no place more closely connected with vampires than these mountains, and there is no one who knows more about them than your uncle. Now that you're old enough, he feels you are ready to join him on one of his expeditions. Your goal: to prove scientifically—once and for all—that vampires exist.

Go on to page 2.

Two other members of the expedition share your compartment on the train: Nina, a blond girl about your age, and Mrs. West, her aunt, a tall and very grand lady in her sixties. Around her neck Mrs. West wears a heavy gold chain. And from the chain dangles the largest jewel you've ever seen. It is a dark blood red, and it seems to glow like a dying fire.

As the train slowly makes its way up and down steep inclines and around tight curves, you take out your uncle's most recent letter and reread the last paragraph:

> Mrs. West and her niece may hold the key to our quest. For generations, their family has kept a painting and a jewel said to possess awesome and terrible powers. If we can use these powers, the painting and jewel should lead us to vampires. If either falls into the wrong hands, we could all be in grave danger. You must protect them and their owners at all costs. But don't worry—you will not be alone in this task. I have helped the Gypsies many times in the past. So wherever you find Gypsies, you will find friends.
>
> Keep safe,
> Andrew

Snow is falling now, and the train moves more and more slowly. In the growing darkness, the fire within Mrs. West's jewel seems to glow brighter and brighter.

Suddenly she jumps to her feet, trembling and

clutching her necklace. "The painting is calling me," she cries. "It's in danger. Someone is after it."

"Oh, Aunt, really," says Nina. "You can't be serious. A painting can't talk."

"Don't be so certain, my dear," says Mrs. West. "I heard it as plainly as I hear you. In any case, I must make sure it's safe." She opens the door and rushes down the corridor toward the baggage car.

Fifteen minutes pass, and Nina begins to look worried. When Mrs. West isn't back after half an hour, she is alarmed. "I'm going after her," she says. "Will you stay here in case I miss her and she returns?" She barely waits for your nod, and then she's running toward the baggage car.

Moments later she's back, wide-eyed and panting. "I can't find her anywhere," she says. "My aunt has vanished."

"I'll help you search the train," you say, trying to stay calm. "Where shall we start?"

"We could go back to the baggage car and look for clues. Or we could ask the other passengers if they've seen her," says Nina. "I'm so worried, I can't think straight. You decide."

If you want to check out the baggage car, turn to page 4.

If you want to question the other passengers, turn to page 31.

4

The baggage car is gloomy and disgusting. Only one dim bulb lights the place, and the car looks as if it hasn't been cleaned in years. Nina gets down on her hands and knees and searches for clues among the dusty old crates, cartons, and suitcases. Meanwhile you try to make sense of the footprints smudged into the grime on the floor. But there's no sign of Mrs. West. She seems to have vanished without a trace.

You're about to give up when Nina calls your name. You make your way through the mess and find her bending over a strange-looking wooden box. "At least we know the painting's safe," says Nina, brushing the dust from her sweater and jeans. "It's kept in this box."

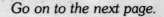

Go on to the next page.

You look closer and see that every inch of the box is covered with carved shapes. There are eyes, ears, mouths, and hands—and they look a little too real for comfort.

"Nina, where did you get this weird thing?" you ask. "Do you know what the carvings mean, or what they have to do with the painting?"

"All I know is that my great-uncle gave it to me before he died," says Nina. "He got it from some relative in Australia, and *she* said it had been in the family almost forever. The box has always been with the painting, and the carvings hide secret locks. My great-uncle showed me how to work them, but I've never actually seen the painting inside."

"Maybe we should look at it now," you say.

"I don't know," says Nina. "Do we have to?"

You show her your uncle's letter. "The painting may help us find your aunt," you say.

"Maybe," she replies, "but what if it *does* have terrible powers, and they turn out to be harmful to us? Maybe we should take your uncle's suggestion and ask the Gypsies for help. We can always come back and open the box later."

If you think it's better to open the box now, turn to page 8.

If you'd rather consult the Gypsies, turn to page 55.

6

At midnight your watch is over. You wake Nanosh and tell him about the little man.

"He could have been a spy," says Nanosh. "And then again it could have been a trap. Maybe the vampires were trying to separate us. Or maybe he really was trying to show us a way into the castle." He's still considering the possibilities when you fall fast asleep.

Laughter! Monstrously loud laughter! Are you dreaming? Someone is shaking your shoulder. "Leave me alone," you shout.

"Wake up, wake up." It's Uncle Andrew. "It will be dawn soon," he says. "I've found a way to open the gate, and I've taken the painting out of its case. We must carry it inside now, so we can attack the monsters at daybreak—when they're most vulnerable."

You sit up, rubbing your eyes. "What time is it?" you ask.

"Nearly six," says Uncle Andrew. "Quickly now, through the gate."

Andrew carries the painting before him like a shield, and you and Nanosh follow close behind. Inside the wall there's a small courtyard, and across the courtyard rises the tower. A stone staircase winds up the outside of the tower wall to a door about halfway to the top. Suddenly the door opens and a light blazes out. Framed against it are a man and woman dressed in evening clothes. The woman wears Mrs. West's jewel, which shines with a horrid red light.

Turn to page 28.

"She went to the baggage car to check on my painting," explains Nina. "When she didn't come back, I went to look for her. But she seems to have disappeared."

"That happens all the time on this train," says the conductor, shaking his head. "Why anyone wants to ride on it, I'll never know."

"Is there anyplace else on the train she could be?" you ask.

"You can look anywhere you like," he says. Then he lowers his voice. "*Except* the private car of Count Zoltan and Countess Carmilla. That is off limits." He backs away, as if in fright. "Few travel in these mountains," he mutters as he retreats. "Do you begin to understand why?"

"I'm not sure I understand at all," you say to Nina, "but it's plain he won't—or can't—give us any help."

"I guess we'll have to ask the other people in the car," says Nina. "Or we can try Count Zoltan's car, even though the conductor said it was off limits."

*If you want to ask the two men for help,
turn to page 12.*

*If you'd like to talk to the Gypsies,
turn to page 55.*

*If you want to knock on Count Zoltan's door,
turn to page 18.*

Once you've decided that the box must be opened, Nina seems to lose her fear. Instead she feels a sudden strange panic to release the painting. Her hands dart frantically over the carvings. She touches an eye here, pulls a finger there, twists an ear. She moves so swiftly, you can hardly see what's happening. Suddenly a crack appears in the side of the box where no seam was visible before, and Nina stumbles backward with a shudder.

"The painting," she whispers. "It wanted me to open the box. It kept making me go faster and faster."

"Do you think it knows we need it?" you ask hopefully.

"I don't know," she replies. "It just wanted to be free."

The box opens slowly—like a clamshell—on invisible hinges, and now you can see the painting that hangs inside. It is a portrait of a handsome man and a beautiful woman, dressed in old-fashioned clothes. A single candle stands on the heavy wooden table between them, its flame casting an eerie light on their faces. Through the open window behind them you can see the full moon.

The painting looks hundreds of years old, and yet the man and woman seem ageless. Their flesh looks real, and their eyes shine with the same glow you saw in Mrs. West's jewel. They seem to stare at you with a terrible, endless hunger.

With great effort you tear your eyes away— and realize that the painting is moving! It strains forward like a leopard ready to pounce on its prey. Then you hear the door of the baggage car open behind you.

Turn to page 48.

Nina has reached the box, and her hands fly over the carvings at an incredible, almost super-human, speed. And now the box is open. And the painting seems to spring out of it and into Nina's arms.

"AIYEEE!" A high-pitched scream blasts through the air. It is Carmilla. She lets go of you, and her hands clutch at her throat, clawing.

And now Zoltan stumbles to a halt. He gasps and gags and begins waving his arms about like a drowning man struggling for air. He staggers backward, recoiling from the painting, and collapses on the floor.

Carmilla, too, is lying in a heap. As you watch, her face and hands soften, like ice melting, and lose their shape. She is melting . . . dissolving . . . and so is the count. You stare, amazed, until nothing remains of the vampires but two oily stains on the floor.

Turn to page 38.

The trap door opens easily, and you look down into a woman's bedroom—only there's a coffin where the bed should be! Heavy floor-to-ceiling drapes cover one wall, shielding the room from any hint of sunlight, and an oil lamp burns on a low table. But the place seems empty, so you leap to the floor, and Nina and Professor Hartz follow.

Whoever lives here is not particularly neat. Even though the room seems to have a closet, there are long dresses heaped on the floor. Out of curiosity, you open the closet door—and find Mrs. West, bound to a chair and gagged.

The three of you untie the ropes and remove the gag. When Mrs. West is completely free, she rises and stamps her foot like a haughty general coming to attention in front of his troops.

Turn to page 96.

Maybe the two men know something that the conductor doesn't. As you enter their compartment, the one in the brightly colored clothes looks up and smiles. He has been playing a game like solitaire, but his deck of cards is far from ordinary. There are strange pictures where the numbers and suits should be.

"My name is Phaino," he says. "And this is Professor Hartz."

Professor Hartz ignores your entrance and the introduction. He is deeply involved in reading an old leather-bound book called *Secrets of the Occult, Volume VII.* When you tell the two men about Mrs. West's disappearance, the professor doesn't seem interested in your problem. He stares out of the window and puffs on his pipe.

Go on to the next page.

Phaino, on the other hand, seems excited by your story. "Perhaps I may be of service," he says. The cards vanish. In their place is a large gold disk with tiny markings on it: letters in some foreign language, animals, suns, and moons.

"Where did the cards go?" you ask.

"Somewhere. Anywhere," he says with a shrug. "You see, I am a maker of dreams and illusions—what some people call a magician." A dove appears in his hand, circles the compartment, and lands on his outstretched wrist. Then it disappears.

"Cheap tricks," sneers the professor. "Games to impress children. Why did Andrew tie me to this brainless prestidigitator?"

"That means magician," Phaino explains, laughing and clapping at the professor's outburst. As he claps, clouds of bright sparks scatter from his hands.

You ask the professor if he's talking about your uncle Andrew, the vampire specialist.

"Of course I mean your uncle," he snaps. "Is there another Andrew in these blasted mountains? He asked me—and that man over there with the ridiculous laugh—to join his vampire expedition. The magician wants to believe that the creatures exist. I will prove, once and for all, that they do not." With that, he stands up and stomps out of the compartment.

Turn to page 66.

The nearest lamp is attached to a bracket on the wall. Casually, you move closer to it, as Nina and Mrs. West open the box. Nina leans the painting against the wall, and the count and countess close in to admire it—which is not surprising, since it's a portrait of *them* painted a long, long time ago. They bend over, pushing Nina and Mrs. West out of the way, to examine every detail.

"Oh, we were so young and fancy-free then!" the countess exclaims, glowing with the memory.

"I *was* a dashing young blade, wasn't I?" says the count, turning to his wife.

"You still are, my love," she replies, smiling fondly.

"A *bloodstained* blade," Mrs. West mutters.

"Now, now, don't be bitter," says the count.

When the vampires' gaze returns to the painting, you brace yourself, wrench the lamp loose, and hurl it at their feet. The lamp bowl shatters as you hoped it would, and kerosene splashes out onto the floor.

You don't wait to see if the oil ignites. You are too busy wrenching another lamp from its fastenings.

"*Fire! Fire!*" the vampires shriek.

The kerosene did ignite! The second lamp is free. You throw it, and the flames spread, easily devouring the cracked, dry wood of the ancient car. Professor Hartz kicks over the wood stove, and burning logs spill onto the floor. The vampires rage and howl, but the flames have created a wall separating them from the four of you.

"Let's go! Quick!" you shout, heading toward the safety of the passenger car.

Turn to page 25.

"I don't think we should wait till morning," you say. "Professor Hartz, will you help us with Nina's plan?"

"Yes," he replies, "in the interest of capturing these thieves and abductors—"

"Vampires," interrupts Mrs. West. "They are *vampires*, Professor."

"Whatever you want to believe, dear lady," he says. "But do let me continue. As I was saying, in the interest of bringing these 'beings' to justice, I will bang on their door and shout that I am a police inspector. I'll say I know Mrs. West is being held prisoner inside."

"Capital idea," Mrs. West says.

And so, while you and Nina climb up to the roof, the professor takes up his station between the passenger car and Count Zoltan's private car. You look down at him and wave. Then you make your way to the rear of the train and down the ladder to the observation platform. No one sees you. So far, so good, you think.

Turn to page 98.

"*Bela!*" The voice comes through the wall—a woman's voice so cold it could freeze an erupting volcano. "Who are you talking to, you nasty thing?"

"Myself!" he shouts back. Then he lowers his voice to a whisper. "That's the countess," he says. "She's always suspicious. Always after me, making my life a misery. I *should* tell her you're here. But it'll serve her right if she has to go hungry." He looks you up and down. "Maybe I'll send you instead."

While you and Nina exchange puzzled glances, Bela scuttles across the floor to his bed. He throws rags left and right. Then he lifts up a floorboard and drags out a large book. The title is *Sorcery for Beginners*.

"*They* don't know about sending," he says maliciously. "Of course, I've never sent humans before. *They're* always too hungry. But I've practiced a lot on sending animals."

"*Sending!*" Professor Hartz exclaims. "What are you talking about?"

"Shhh!" Bela hisses. "You'll have her in here. Then I'll get in trouble." He flips through the book's musty pages, finding his place. "Now, tell me where you want to go," he says. "Then I'll try to send you there. But pick someplace easy. Sorcery's kind of unreliable. You may end up where you don't expect to."

Turn to page 77.

"You knock on the door of Count Zoltan's car, but no one answers. You knock again, harder, and after a time the door swings open. A fat, dwarfish man with a puffy, repulsive face stands there scowling.

"Go away," he growls.

"We're looking for my aunt, Mrs. West," Nina says politely. "Have you by any—"

"*Go away!*" he interrupts. "You don't want to be here."

Turn to page 103.

Bela chants words in a language you've never heard: Grotchik Bela spavivi joi; Boska neer, Lola feer, Andra seer!

And in less time than it takes to change channels on TV, you find yourself on the beach of a lush and lovely tropical island. Nina is next to you, blinking in surprise. On your other side is Professor Hartz, looking startled and disbelieving. A few feet up the beach—bound, gagged, and tied to a chair—is Mrs. West. She makes frantic sounds, and Nina quickly runs over to release her.

But the biggest surprise of all is emerging from the blue waters of the lagoon: Uncle Andrew, thrashing about and spluttering and looking terribly uncomfortable in his winter clothes.

"I'm delighted to see you," Andrew says when he finally manages to clamber up onto the beach. "But what in thunder's going on?"

You try to explain about the vampires and Bela and the sending. "But I still don't know how we got here," you finish.

"Even though every bone in my body cries out against it," says the professor, "I'd have to say it is sorcery."

"It can be nothing else," Uncle Andrew says. "In any case, wherever it is we are, let's make the best of it. I have the feeling that we'll be here for quite a long time." Then he turns to you and Nina and asks, "Have either of you read *Robinson Crusoe* lately?"

The End

"Cut that out!" you say. "I don't want to be hypnotized."

Phaino shakes his head sadly and puts away the disk. "Oh, dear," he says. "I was only trying to help. I hoped to let you sleep and forget. You would have arrived at your destination safe and sound."

"But what about my aunt?" Nina asks, waking up.

"I was coming to that." Phaino's face is troubled. "Since you will not travel safely the way of sleep and dreams, you will have to journey the other way."

"The other way?" you ask.

"The way of terror . . . or worse! In the end you *may* find your aunt," he says to Nina, "and she *may* be safe. . . ."

A chipmunk peers out from under Phaino's coat collar. It takes a look around, then disappears. The magician jumps to his feet, suddenly enthusiastic. "Meanwhile, we must prepare carefully," he says. "I have created a new device—a vampire trap. Unfortunately, it has never been tested."

He takes down a large metal locker from the rack above his seat. He opens it and removes several odd-shaped packages. Then the three of you go to the baggage car, where he unpacks several large mirrors.

As Phaino bustles about setting up the trap, he explains the theory behind it. The device is a combination of mirrors and red, green, and blue lasers. In ordinary light, vampires don't cast reflections in mirrors, nor do they cast shadows. But lasers don't make ordinary light.

"If I can catch the vampires' reflections," says

Phaino, "then I can catch *them*. The mirrors are set up facing each other, and the lasers will shine from the outside. If we can draw the vampires between the mirrors, they will be ours!"

Suddenly you hear the sound of someone running. It's Mrs. West! "Help me, please!" she cries. "The vampires are after me. I escaped, but they're coming after me!"

Turn to page 117.

The snow is coming down very hard when you reach the station, but none of you is sorry to leave the train. You find a telephone inside, and after several tries you finally reach your uncle. He tells you to take the painting to the inn in a nearby village and wait for him there.

The snow ends early the next morning, and the sun comes out. But the temperature remains well below freezing. In the afternoon Andrew arrives on horseback, leading mounts for you and the others and a pack horse for supplies, equipment, and the painting.

When you last saw him, your uncle was clean-shaven. Now he has a bushy silver beard. Otherwise he's exactly as you remember him: short, red-faced, and plump, with a fringe of white hair around his bald dome. Although he appears jolly and friendly, there is steel in his eyes. As soon as he dismounts, he fixes those strong, piercing eyes on Nina. "We'll do our very best to find and rescue your aunt," he promises. Then he turns to you and adds, "And I believe we will soon have proof of the existence of vampires."

A few minutes later the four of you are on your horses, riding single file up a dangerously steep and narrow mountain trail. Later, in a dark wooded valley, you hear snarls and howls behind you. You turn in your saddle. There are dozens of gray shapes loping through the trees.

"Wolves!" says Nanosh.

Turn to page 40.

The three of you race to the baggage car. Although there is little light and the car is a cluttered, dirty mess, you have no trouble finding the box that holds the painting. It would be hard to miss, with its strange, intricate carvings of hands, eyes, ears, and mouths. With Nanosh as guard, you and Nina carry the box back to the Gypsies' compartment.

Lyuba breathes a sigh of relief when she sees you. Then she explains her urgency. "There is a private car, attached to this train, that belongs to Count Zoltan and Countess Carmilla," she says. "If you were to open the box, you would behold a painting of them as they were centuries ago— when they were young and mortal. Now they are unaging creatures of the dark."

"Vampires!" says Nanosh.

"The painting can release forces that will be their undoing," continues Lyuba. "But we cannot use it here, where their power is strong. We must journey to our camp and communicate with the Old Ones. They will tell us what to do."

"What about my aunt?" Nina asks.

"And what about the jewel?" you chime in. "Uncle Andrew said it was powerful, too."

"Of the jewel, I know nothing," says Lyuba. "But I will ask the Old Ones about it also. Now come, make ready. We will leave the train at the next station." She strokes Nina's cheek with her gnarled old hand. "This is your aunt's only hope," she says gently.

Turn to page 64.

The two vampires *love* the brighter beams. And now they are waltzing!

As they dance, you find yourself staring at the count. For an instant you meet the deathly black void of his gaze. The eyes lock onto you, command you not to move. And when they swing away, you find yourself paralyzed.

Turn to page 118.

Moments later, the four of you step aboard the passenger car. Then Nina helps her aunt down the corridor and into her compartment while you and Professor Hartz free the couplings that fasten Count Zoltan's car to the rest of the train.

Not a second too soon. As the train pulls away, a huge ball of fire engulfs the car. The blast that follows is so tremendous it almost shakes the train from the tracks.

When the train stops vibrating, you look back once more. Nothing remains but a crater. There's no trace of the count's car—not even smoke.

"They've gone," you say to the professor. "Not even vampires could survive that explosion."

"Vampires?" the professor says. "You still believe that those two were vampires?"

"Yes, I do," you say firmly.

"Hmmpf!" he replies. Then he smiles for the first time since you met him. "Well, whatever they were, they were up to no good. And I daresay that the world is well rid of them."

The End

"Let's get out of here—fast," you yell to Nina.

"All right," she says. "But . . ."

"No buts. Come *on!*" you insist, tugging at her arm. "We'll go up to the engine and ask for help there."

The two of you run to the door of the baggage car. Lost as they are in the pleasures of dancing, the vampires don't seem to notice. But when you reach the door, Nina jerks your hand away from the handle.

"Stop," she says. "We can't leave the painting. It's calling me again."

"Nina, don't be silly," you say. "That voice is all in your imagination."

"It's *not* my imagination," she insists. "It's as real as you and me. Please! Help me with the painting. Trust me."

If you make Nina come with you to the engine, turn to page 88.

If you agree to go back to the painting, turn to page 114.

The Gypsies' compartment is warm and cosy. You introduce yourselves, and the Gypsies tell you their names. The young man is Nanosh, a Gypsy prince. He wears a bright green shirt with wide, puffy sleeves, and a green-and-blue-striped bandanna on his head. The old woman is Lyuba. She has on a blue-and-gold striped skirt, a soft red wool sweater, and a black shawl. She has clipped three fresh blue flowers in her beautiful white hair, and she looks very wise and kind.

The Gypsies don't seem terribly interested when Nina tells them of her aunt's disappearance. But when you mention your uncle Andrew, their eyes light up.

"Andrew has saved my life more than once," Nanosh says. "Anything we can do for you will scarcely begin to repay his love for us."

"Yes, we will help you in every way we can. However," Lyuba says gravely, "this train is not safe. I feel evil in the air. And worse than evil—vampires are near."

Turn to page 39.

"Count Zoltan and Countess Carmilla," whispers Nanosh.

"Welcome to our home," says the count. "We thought you might try to approach us at this hour. But don't you know that the painting is now helpless against us? My wife wears the Bloodstone, the precious jewel that was lost to us these many centuries. It is the one thing that can protect us from the painting. You are dead, mortal fools!"

Andrew seems to be trembling with fright. But then you realize it's the painting that's shaking. "Hurry," he gasps. "Grab the painting. Hold tight."

You and Nanosh rush to his side and grasp the frame. The painting feels alive. It bucks like a horse. Then streaks of colored light leap from its surface, surrounding it in a whirlpool of lightning. Gold, silver, violet, green, and blue lightning bolts strike out at the vampires. But the red glow from the Bloodstone not only protects them like a force field, it batters the blazing light back toward the painting. The evil red glow closes in, presses down.

Turn to page 63.

Somehow you shift your weight to your other foot, and the step tilts back like a stone seesaw. You are safe—but for how long? You take a deep breath and go on.

At the top of the staircase there's a door that opens into a luxurious room brightly lit by candles. Count Zoltan and Countess Carmilla are seated at a dining table. No food is before them, but one place across from them is set for supper. The two smile graciously.

"You are to be congratulated," says Carmilla. "You are the first mortal to survive the Corridor of Death."

"Yes," says Zoltan. "The others died of fright. Can you imagine?" He chuckles. "Please sit down. We have prepared supper for you."

"No thanks," you say.

"Too bad," Carmilla sighs. "You have a long journey before you."

"You are strong," says Zoltan, "strong enough to survive the terrors of the corridor. We do not destroy the strong. But we cannot allow you to remember us." He rises from his chair and lifts his arms high over his head. The room grows dark . . .

. . . And you are at home, watching TV. On the screen, four horseback riders follow a narrow road through gloomy mountains. Soon you see that the road leads to an ancient, ruined castle. You've seen that castle before. You've been there. You *know* you have. But when? And how? The memory eludes you.

The End

The two of you step out into the corridor and look up and down. Mrs. West made sure you had a pretty nice compartment, but the rest of the train looks so old and worn out, you wonder how it holds together at all. Nina shivers. "It's really cold in here," she says.

"Let's get moving," you reply. "Maybe that will warm us up."

It appears that there are few others riding on the train. In one compartment are two Gypsies, a handsome young man and an extremely old woman. In another, two men sit opposite each other. One is tall and distinguished looking. He wears a brown plaid suit and smokes a curved stem pipe. The other is small and nervous looking and wears strange, brightly colored clothes.

The other compartments are empty. Ahead of your car are the baggage car, the coal car, and the engine. Behind you is another car, but the door to it is locked.

You meet the conductor in the corridor. He does not look friendly.

"Have you seen my aunt, Mrs. West?" Nina asks.

"No," he says, averting his eyes.

Turn to page 7.

When you reach the gate of the ruined castle, you discover it is closed tight and locked.

"Strike the gate with Luluvo's Star," Nanosh suggests.

You do that, and the crystal emits a pure, lovely tone. At once the gate swings open, revealing a small courtyard. On the opposite side of the courtyard there's a tower.

"Okay," you say, gathering up your courage. "I guess we'd better go in."

"Wait," says Nina. "I think it's time to remove the painting from its box." She places it carefully on the ground and then releases the locks and latches hidden in the intricate carvings. Once the painting is out in the open, it seems to come alive. It practically pulls Nina to a doorway in the tower. The door leads to a stone staircase, and the stairs descend into the dark.

You and the Gypsies light torches and slowly, cautiously make your way down the worn, ancient staircase. At the bottom you find yourselves in a huge, vaulted room carved out of mountain bedrock. It is empty. You pass through an arched doorway and into a dark, narrow tunnel. Shadows flicker ominously in the torchlit gloom.

For miles, it seems, the tunnel slopes deeper and deeper into the mountain. Finally you enter another room . . . a room that's exactly like your own room at home!

Turn to page 112.

Cautiously you open the second door. What you find behind it is more a closet than a room . . . more a den for a wild animal than a sleeping place for a human being.

In a corner on the floor is an old-fashioned, wind-up phonograph, playing a recording of the most pitiful, heart-rending animal noises you've ever heard. Bent over the phonograph is a squat, dwarfish, repulsive-looking man. He is so intent on listening, he doesn't hear you. In another corner there's a jumble of rags where the little man seems to make his bed. Old, gnawed-on bones litter the floor. And here and there you see green and rotting globs of stuff you'd rather not identify.

"I say," says Professor Hartz, trying to catch the man's attention.

"Quiet," he replies. "Don't bother me. I'm listening."

When the record is finally over, he turns toward you. "Well," he says, "I suppose you want to know about the count and countess and that old lady they snatched."

"Mrs. West?" you say. "Then she is here."

"Right in the next room, tied up," says the little man. "The count's off to the baggage car to grab that painting and jewel they want so badly. And the countess is lying down in the parlor, probably dreaming about how thirsty she is. Maybe I should tell her you're here, especially seeing as how you're all so full of nice rich human blood."

Turn to page 17.

There are a number of cans in your saddlebag. You reach inside, pull one out, and heave it at the leader of the pack. It hits him on the head, just behind the ears. "Get out of here," you shout, waving your arms. You pull out another can, and another. Miraculously, most of your shots find their mark, and the wolves slink away, dazed and frightened.

"Help!" a voice cries from the tree. It's Nina.

"Are you okay?" you ask, helping her down.

"I don't know," she replies. "I hurt my leg climbing the tree."

There's a rip in her jeans, and under the tear there's a bloody scrape.

"This looks bad," you say. "Maybe we should ride back to town and have it looked at by a doctor."

"No!" she cries. "There's no time for that. We have to catch up to Andrew and Nanosh. They have the painting, and that's the key to finding my aunt."

"But your leg needs treatment," you argue.

"I have peroxide and bandages in my pack. Come on. Help me find my horse. Then let's get going."

Turn to page 102.

You and Nina are very worried about Mrs. West. But Phaino is excited and bubbly now that he knows the vampires are actually nearby. "This is the chance of a lifetime," he says gleefully.

You turn to talk to Nina, but she is off in a corner, staring at a wooden box covered with weird carvings. "The painting is inside this box," she says, beckoning you. "I think it's trying to tell me something."

You study your friend with growing concern. A painting that talks? Is she going crazy?

"There," she whispers excitedly. "There it is again. Don't you hear it?"

The only sounds you hear are the train's movements and Phaino adjusting his equipment.

"Oh, I don't know if I can," Nina says to the box. She backs away from it, her hands trembling, her eyes wide with fear. "Ohhh . . . I . . . it . . ." she gasps.

"Please, my dear. Please don't be frightened," Phaino breaks in. He stops fiddling with his device. "Come on. We can't just sit around and terrify ourselves waiting. Soon the vampires will be snared in my trap, and all will be well," he says cheerfully. "Here, watch."

He waves his arms, and a fire-breathing dragon flies through the air with a beautiful maiden in its claws. "Oh, I'm terribly sorry, I forgot," he says, smiling. And now there's a knight in silver armor racing after the dragon. Then Phaino pulls a long rope of saltwater taffy from your ear and gold coins from under Nina's tongue.

You hear applause; then a woman speaks. "How amazing these human tricks are. They're

almost as good as the real thing.'' It is the countess. In a flash she's a bat, and just as quickly she's a woman again. Then she slowly walks toward the three of you, gazing at you the way a shark gazes at a particularly tasty fish.

Turn to page 49.

You'd like to sit down and catch your breath, but in storms Mrs. West.

"Nina!" she yells. "I am *not* pleased with you. You did *not* come to my assistance. Instead, you left me in the clutches of those repellant creatures."

"But, Aunt," Nina pleads. "They're gone now. They're dead. We won."

"You did? You won?" Mrs. West says.

"Yes!" says Nina. "The painting destroyed them."

"Well . . . um . . . uh . . . yes. Good," says Mrs. West in a calmer voice. "But where is the painting, then? And my jewel?"

Nina looks puzzled, for the painting has vanished from her hands—and the carved box along with it. And though you search the baggage car from top to bottom, you also fail to find the jewel. Even though Mrs. West insists time and again that this is where she hid it, the necklace has vanished.

Baffled, the three of you are about to go back to your compartment, when you notice Phaino, slumped across his control panel.

"Phaino!" Nina cries. "Are you okay?"

The little man's eyes open a crack, and he takes a quick, furtive look around. "Are they gone?" he whispers.

"Yes," you answer. "They're gone forever."

"Fine . . . no, terrific!" Phaino says, brightening. "Then my device *did* work, after all. You are truly fortunate that I was here to help!"

Nina catches your eye, and you both laugh until you cry.

The End

Lyuba turns her face toward the ceiling and closes her eyes. For a long moment she stays like that, listening to something none of you can hear. "There's a painting in a carved wooden box in the baggage car," she says at last. "You know of it?"

Nina nods. "It belongs to me and my aunt," she says.

"The painting is the key. It can destroy the vampires," says Lyuba. "But we must not stay here. We will take the painting to our camp and consult the Old Ones. They will tell us how to use the painting and how to rescue Mrs. West."

The professor rises. "I believe you are good people," he says to the Gypsies, "but it is obvious that you are misguided, the victims of a serious delusion. The evidence indicates that Mrs. West has been captured by thieves who want her valuable red jewel. To leave the train now, when Mrs. West—and the scoundrels—may still be nearby, is an act of folly. We must search the train for clues."

You're not sure you agree with the professor's theory about jewel thieves. But he may have a point about leaving the train.

If you go with the Gypsies to their camp, turn to page 64.

If you remain on the train to search for clues with Professor Hartz, turn to page 71.

The wolves are getting closer, and your horse snorts with fear.

"We'll have to run for it," says Uncle Andrew.

You spur your horses toward the end of the woods and safety. Behind you, you hear a horse stumble; then there's a muffled thud. But you don't realize what's happened until Nina's riderless horse canters up beside you.

"Stop!" you shout. "Nina's been thrown."

The three of you rein in your horses and swing around. But you can't see a thing. Between the time you spotted the wolves and the moment you turned back for Nina, a mysterious, thick cloud has blanketed the woods.

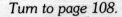

Turn to page 108.

Hiding all night behind the curtains is quite an experience. You've heard of horses sleeping on their feet, but you never knew humans could—until you tried it yourself. Each of you takes a turn keeping watch, and finally dawn comes.

While the others untie Mrs. West again, you check Carmilla's coffin. It's empty—something that surprises everyone but the professor.

"Perhaps she has other resting places," suggests Mrs. West. "We will search all the rooms in this infernal place; the vampires must be somewhere."

You go through the car from top to bottom, but the place is deserted. No count. No countess. No servant. No jewel. No painting.

"The vampires have escaped with what they wanted most," Mrs West says, sighing deeply.

"Madam, they are not vampires," says the professor. "They are thieves . . . kidnappers . . . no more, no less."

But you *know* they are vampires. And now, with the Bloodstone and the painting in their grasp, they are infinitely more dangerous than they were before. Perhaps Uncle Andrew will have a plan that can lead to their destruction. You hope so. But for now, there's nothing more to do.

The End

Bela mutters weird-sounding words in a strange language: Grotchik Bela spavivi xloi; Spasha kom, Lasha dom, Masha hom!

There's a burst of light . . . and you find yourselves in a sandy, rocky wasteland beneath a blinding, seering sun. Striding toward you is a towering, muscular man. He is bare to the waist and carries a long black bullwhip. He flicks his whip casually as he approaches.

"Ho, ho, ho," he laughs. "Newcomers to the Slavepits of Hom. Welcome and kneel."

The Slavepits of Hom! This wasn't the "home" you had in mind.

"Kneel!" roars the man, and he cracks the whip across your back. You kneel.

"Girl, kneel." Nina kneels.

"Man, kneel." Professor Hartz kneels.

"Old woman, kneel." You hadn't realized it till now, but poor old Mrs. West was sent to Hom with you. She is bound and gagged and tied to a chair. But somehow or other she manages to pitch herself forward, chair and all.

"Here are my rules," the giant continues, cracking his whip. "They are simple; remember them. You dig for the diamonds that lie within the soil. When you find one, you bring it to me. Sometimes as you dig you will find water. That you may drink. Other times you will find worms. Those you may eat. Do not try to escape. There is no escape from Hom."

The End

Uncle Andrew examines Mrs. West closely. "She's not dead," he says, "But she is in some kind of a trance. I think she will be all right once we've dealt with the count and countess. Nina, will you remove the painting from its case?"

While Nina unlocks the secret latches and fastenings, you examine Zoltan and Carmilla. He is handsome and she is beautiful, and yet, even in sleep, they are repulsive. Their rest is not like human sleep at all. They do not breathe; they appear truly dead. Carmilla's hands are wrapped tight as steel bands around Mrs. West's jewel. It glows a dark evil red.

Nina lifts the painting from its case . . . and it emerges like the sun at dawn, blazing with a light so bright it engulfs the jewel's red glow as easily as the sun dims a candle.

For a moment the vampires seem to awaken and breathe. Then their faces go ashen, and they howl from the depths of their horrid souls.

The vampires' faces and hands crease and shrivel as though they were aging a decade each minute. Then their bodies begin to shrink. They grow smaller and smaller until, at last, nothing is left of them.

When the final drop of blood seeps from the coffins, Mrs. West wakes and sits up. "Well," she says with a scowl, "it's about time. I thought you'd never come!"

The End

You move as fast as you can, but you're too late. The little man cries out. Then he dives on top of you and Nina, pinning you down. He is stronger than he looks.

"Good! Good! Two more," says a man who has just entered the room. He is, no doubt, the count. He is dressed in expensive evening clothes—and he carries Professor Hartz like a sack of groceries. Behind him follows a woman—the countess—carrying Mrs. West. "You have done well, Bela," the count continues. "Now you may let the mortals rise."

You and Nina stand up, and the vampires dump the professor and Nina's aunt next to you. Then the count picks up Mrs. West's necklace and clasps the gold chain around the countess's neck. He steps back, beaming with admiration. "At last, the Bloodstone is where it belongs," he says. "And now, to the painting. Which of you will open the case for me?" No one moves. "Come now," he says with menace in his voice. "Do I have to force you?"

Turn to page 85.

Lyuba hurls the crimson stone into the heart of the fire. Thunder roars. Huge clouds of red smoke surge from the flames and cover her completely.

After a time she emerges and approaches you, her arms outstretched. "The Old Ones have spoken again," she says. "They say that you have become one with us, that wherever you go, you will always find a home among Gypsies. But this country is no longer safe for you. You must leave and never return. The vampires possess the Bloodstone, the jewel they took from Mrs. West. With it they are more dangerous than ever."

"Does that mean my aunt is dead?" Nina asks, her voice trembling.

"The Old Ones believe she lives—and there is hope she may yet be saved," Lyuba replies. "More than anything else in the world, the vampires want to own the painting *and* the Bloodstone. If you are willing to give up the painting in exchange for your aunt, we will approach the count and see if he is willing to accept such a bargain."

"But if they have the painting and the jewel, won't the vampires be invulnerable?" you ask.

"No one who must shun the light of day is invulnerable," says Nanosh. "With the help of the Old Ones, we will yet destroy our enemies."

For a moment Nina holds her breath, deciding. Then she nods. "Yes, yes! Trade it. What's a painting compared to my aunt's life?"

"If that is your wish, we will attempt to grant it. Meanwhile Nanosh will take you to Budapest. If all goes well, Mrs. West will join you there."

A few days after you arrive in Budapest, Mrs. West *does* show up. You find her waiting for you in the ornate lobby of the Hotel Grand National. Standing alongside her is Uncle Andrew. You can't wait to talk to him. Maybe you don't have scientific proof that vampires exist, but you certainly have enough proof to convince yourself.

The End

The door of the baggage car closes, and the painting is suddenly still. You turn around, hoping, to find Mrs. West, but instead you see a young man. He is wearing a bright green shirt with wide, puffy sleeves; a green-and-blue-striped bandanna is tied around his head.

"I am Nanosh, prince of the Gypsies," says the young man.

"Then you must know my uncle Andrew," you say.

"More than that, I owe him my life," Nanosh says simply. "He asked me to watch out for you and those who accompany you, and to protect the painting in their possession. You must need me now, because the painting has called."

Nina tells Nanosh about her missing aunt and about the jewel.

"According to Uncle Andrew, it, too, is supposed to have great powers," you say.

"I know nothing of this jewel," says Nanosh, "but of the painting I can speak. We have many legends of its magic, and your uncle believes that it can destroy vampires. The man in the picture is Count Zoltan, the woman is his wife, Carmilla. I have discovered that they are on this very train, in their own private car. So you and the painting are in grave danger." He lowers his voice. "My people say they are vampires. You must leave the train at once."

Turn to page 86.

Countess Carmilla stops when she comes to the vampire trap Phaino has made. "With *this* you intend to capture us?" Laughing, she places a hand in front of one of the mirrors. The hand makes no reflection. "When will you turn it on?" she asks. "I can't wait."

Her teasing doesn't seem to bother Phaino. He runs over to his control panel and starts flipping switches and turning knobs. But Nina is angry. Her fists are clenched, and her face is red.

"Where is my aunt?" she shouts. "Bring her back! Right now!"

"No, my dear. I'm afraid I can't do that. But I do think I will let you see your aunt after supper."

Nina screams and rushes at the vampire with fists flying. Her attack is so fierce and sudden that she knocks the countess flat on her back.

"Stop her, quickly!" Phaino pleads. "She'll ruin everything."

Do you pull Nina away, or do you help her attack Carmilla? You have only a split second to decide.

If you join the fight, turn to page 70.

*If you stop Nina and follow Phaino's plan,
turn to page 74.*

You creep around the corner where you last saw the ugly little man, and the beam of your flashlight catches him opening a small door into the castle. When you reach it, you find the door isn't locked. So you open it—cautiously—and enter a narrow corridor with a ceiling so low, you have to bend your head.

The door slams behind you, and you hear an unpleasant barking laugh. You are about to investigate who—or what—it is, when something snatches your flashlight and hurls it with tremendous force against the wall.

Dark! Darkness blacker than the tombs.

You whirl around. Behind you there's a pair of red eyes. Then a second pair. Then a third. And a hideous, poisonous stench—like rotting meat. Blindly you blunder forward, keeping one hand on the wall for guidance.

The red eyes follow.

You reach a stairway and begin to climb. It's a steep, twisting spiral, which is a relief because the turns block out the red eyes. You climb higher, and now the staircase no longer has an outer wall. There is only a terrifying, endless opening, and you sense deep, empty spaces beneath you. From far below rises a terrible noise, like large creatures in violent combat, thrashing about in a pool of water.

You climb on. Your foot presses down on a stone step, and the step tilts—toward the deep, empty space. . . .

Turn to page 30.

"Nina! Nina, wake up!" you say urgently. You grab her shoulders and shake her.

Phaino looks up, startled.

"What? What did you say?" Nina asks, bleary-eyed and cotton headed.

"I said wake up. We've got to get out of here," you say. "He's trying to hypnotize us."

Phaino bows his head sadly as you take hold of Nina's wrists and pull her out the door. The wintry air in the corridor wakes both of you like a cold bath.

"What now?" you ask Nina, staring out into the snowstorm.

"I don't know," she replies.

"May I join you?" the professor says, approaching you from the end of the corridor.

"Please do," says Nina. "I just don't know what to do."

"Well, I wouldn't say that," he replies. "You certainly did the right thing in leaving that man Phaino. He is not to be trusted. If you continue to think clearly and logically, I *see* no reason why you shouldn't find your aunt."

"Can *you* help, then?" she asks.

"I can certainly try," he assures her. "Without a doubt, your aunt's disappearance can be explained by natural causes. The first that occurs to me is thieves. This country is full of thieves. Was the lady wearing any jewelry?"

"Only a large red stone on a chain," Nina answers. "But I never thought of it as valuable."

"Ahh, but it *may* be worth very much, in which case your aunt would be a prime target for thieves," says the professor. "However, thieves always leave footprints . . . fingerprints . . . things like that. It is their nature to do so. If we search for clues and question the other people on the train, I'm positive we'll soon be hot on her trail—er—as they say."

Nina is shaking her head in doubt, but neither of you can offer another plan.

"Good," says the professor, rubbing his hands in anticipation. "Where shall we begin?"

If you decide to question the Gypsies, turn to page 27.

If you decide to search the baggage car, turn to page 56.

If you decide to look for clues in the passenger car, turn to page 71.

"You go on ahead, and we'll join you as soon as we can," you say, hoping you sound more confident than you feel. Then, while Andrew and Nanosh resume the mission, you continue to search for Nina.

The fog is incredibly thick now. If you didn't know you were breathing, you could easily believe you were underwater. Off to one side you can hear wolves snarling and snapping. Carefully you approach. The noise grows louder and uglier, and then you are upon them. They have surrounded a tree and are leaping at the lower branches, yapping frantically.

Turn to page 35.

You knock on the door of the Gypsies' compartment, and a lady with blue flowers clipped to her beautiful white hair beckons you inside. She is very old and yet ageless, and she looks wise and kindly. Across from her sits a young man wearing a bright green shirt with wide, puffy sleeves and a green-and-blue-striped bandanna on his head. When you introduce yourselves, you discover that the young man is Nanosh, prince of the Gypsies, and the lady's name is Lyuba.

"So Andrew is your uncle," Nanosh says, looking impressed. "He is a great and close friend, and he has saved my life more than once." He looks at Nina's troubled face. "You have sought us for some reason," he says. "How can we help you?"

Nina explains that she and her aunt were carrying a red jewel and a painting to Andrew for use in his quest for vampires. But now her aunt has disappeared.

"Is the painting kept in a carved wooden box?" Lyuba asks.

"Why, yes," Nina answers. "How did you know?"

"Our people have known of the painting for centuries," says Nanosh.

Lyuba clutches Nina's wrist. "Go—quickly! Bring the painting here," she says. "Do not lose a second. I will explain why after you return. Nanosh, go with them—for protection."

Turn to page 23.

The baggage car is nearly dark. The only light comes from a dim bulb hanging near the middle of the car—and from what appears to be a small red lantern someone is carrying up near the front.

"I say . . ." calls out Professor Hartz, but his voice is lost in a sudden blast of wind that sweeps down the car. The person up ahead has opened the door. For a moment he stands in the doorway, and you can see he is carrying a large wooden box.

"Shhh, Professor," Nina whispers. "I think that red light comes from my aunt's jewel. Somehow that man has gotten hold of it, and he has our painting, too!"

While the man reaches out for the ladder that leads up to the roof, you quickly tell the professor what your uncle said about the painting and the jewel. "We have to follow that man," you say.

"Has he seen us?" Nina asks.

"Let's hope not," you say, "but we'll find out soon enough."

"Do the two of you realize that following him means going up onto the roof of a moving train— in a blizzard?" the professor asks.

"He may lead us to my aunt," Nina says.

"We don't have any choice," you say, rushing toward the other end of the car.

Turn to page 72.

Doors open and people enter the square. They shuffle toward you like zombies in a movie. Their faces are dull and lifeless.

"Who are they? They're horrible!" Nina gasps, clutching Mrs. West's hand.

"Many years ago, these people tried to revolt against me," says Zoltan. "As a . . . reward . . . I gave them death in life, forever—a reward you four will share." He turns back toward the train. "Good-bye," he says, laughing, "and have a nice day."

The four of you look for a way to escape, a place to run to. But the villagers surround you. Pale white faces come closer and closer. Lifeless hands reach out for you.

The End

The three of you put your shoulders to the door and shove hard. To your surprise, it pops open, and you see a dimly lit corridor. When you step inside, you hear weird and terrifying noises, like jungle animals in pain. Only the determined look on Nina's face keeps you from turning around and going back.

There are a couple of doors off the corridor. You put your ear to the first—and hear nothing. Just an ominous silence. Could Mrs. West be behind that door? The frightening noises seem to be coming from the second door. Oh, no! you think. What if she's in there!

You give the professor and Nina a questioning look. They both shrug. The choice is up to you.

If you try the first door, turn to page 76.

If you try the second door, turn to page 34.

You're running out of time—but suddenly Nina catches on. She gives you a tiny wink and the whisper of a smile. "How could I forget *The Pink Panther*?" she says.

The vampires' eyes are still drinking in the painting as Nina nudges up close to Carmilla, as if she wanted a better look at it herself. And then the jewel is in her hand. She jerks hard. It's free!

"Throw it here!" you yell.

She throws, and in one smooth move you catch the jewel and fling it through the hole in the glass. The Bloodstone sails out into the night.

The vampires shriek and strike out at you. But they seem to have become blind.

"Look at the painting," the professor cries.

The eyes of the couple in the portrait are on fire! Four flaming ribbons spill out of those eyes and wind around the vampires until they are engulfed in cocoons of fire.

"Move quickly," says the professor. "The flames will spread."

The four of you dash forward to the passenger car and manage to uncouple the burning car before it can ignite the rest of the train. As you leave Count Zoltan and Countess Carmilla behind, huge spurts of flame pour out of the old wooden car into the snowy night. You're sorry the painting and the Bloodstone are lost, but you're pretty sure Uncle Andrew will approve of what you've done.

"*Now* do you believe in vampires?" Mrs. West asks Professor Hartz.

He nods his head, but only barely.

The End

"The pastries *do* look delicious," Nina says.

"And I think I might try the cookies," you say.

"Do! Do!" the count says. "And you *must* taste some of the red fruit punch. My wife makes it herself, and I can assure you, there's nothing like it on this earth."

It turns out that the cookies don't taste as good as they look. They're stale and musty in your mouth—like old mushrooms. And when you swallow a bite, you start to feel an odd tingle that you don't like at all. You spit out what's left and grab Nina's hand. "Don't eat any more," you yell. "Run!"

The count blocks the door to the corridor. He smiles broadly, and you catch a glimpse of dagger-sharp white teeth.

Vampires!

Turn to page 87.

You and Nina climb up the stairs to the tower door and enter the vampires' lair. You pass through corridor after corridor, room after room. There's no sign of Mrs. West, and the air is suffocating and damp.

"This place is incredible," says Nina. "From the outside it looks small, but inside it goes on and on."

"Yeah," you reply. "I feel like a rat in a maze. Your aunt could be three feet away and we would still miss her. Let's retrace our steps and go find Uncle Andrew. He'll know what to do."

But that proves to be impossible. You are lost. The only thing you can do is keep going.

After a time you find yourself in an empty, windowless room—just like so many others you've already passed through. But this one proves to be different. . . .

The door closes behind you. You run over and try to open it, but it's locked! Has someone been following you? That's alarming enough. But what really scares you is the ceiling: it seems to be descending. And now the floor shudders and starts to rise. At the rate of a foot a minute, you figure the floor and ceiling will meet in eight minutes.

The End

"The painting needs more help from us," Andrew shouts. "You must *believe* you can win! You must *trust* the powers the painting can release!"

You *do* believe you can stop the vampires. You concentrate your entire being on the thought. And the spreading flood of red light slows . . . stops. It's a standoff, and it seems to go on forever.

All of you—humans *and* vampires—are so locked in battle, you don't notice the arrival of day until the sun rises over the castle wall and fills the courtyard with brilliant light. The painting seems to drink it in. The jewel grows dull, and the red glow fades.

Now the vampires are terrified. They try to retreat into their tower. But before they can escape, two brilliant bolts of pure white energy surge from the painting. There's a tremendous blast and two white flashes . . . and where the vampires once stood there's nothing but sulpherous smoke.

Turn to page 80.

The snow is falling heavily when you reach the next stop, and the station is cold and dark. But your heart lifts as you watch the train pull away. Vampires or no vampires, something about that train made your skin crawl. It was like a haunted house on wheels.

Nanosh gives one of the village boys a silver coin to take a message to the Gypsy camp. "By morning we will have transport," he says cheerfully. Then he stokes up the wood stove in the station, and the four of you sleep as best you can.

When you wake in the morning, the snow has stopped and a pair of horse-drawn carts has arrived to carry you and the painting to the Gypsy camp. That night there is feasting, singing, dancing, and storytelling. Then, at midnight, everyone falls silent and Lyuba goes into a deep trance.

"What is she doing?" you whisper to Nanosh.

"Hush," he whispers back. "She is talking to the Old Ones. They will tell us what to do."

After a time, Lyuba rises from her trance and comes to stand in front of you. She removes two brightly polished egg-shaped stones from a leather pouch that dangles from a thong around her neck. One of the stones is crimson; the other is emerald green.

"The Old Ones have spoken," she says in a deep, level voice. "You must decide which of these stones is to be transformed by fire. Choose the crimson, and you will find both safety and a satisfactory conclusion to your search. Choose the green, and you risk terrible failure and a dire fate; but your success, should you win it, will be beyond your greatest dreams." She thrusts the stones toward you. "Choose," she cries.

If you pick the crimson stone, turn to page 46.

If you pick the emerald-green stone, turn to page 100.

The magician is suddenly serious. "But there *are* vampires," he says, "and I fear they are very close. But all will be well if you study this disk." His voice is calm and soothing, and the gold disk flashes on and off in the light, now shining, now dark. "We will find Mrs. West. She will be safe. You will be safe . . . safe . . . safe . . ."

You find yourself growing sleepy. You give Nina a little shove, but she is fast asleep. Phaino has hypnotized her, and you feel you are in danger of falling into a trance, too. With your last bit of strength, you could wake Nina and try to escape from Phaino. Or you could grab his gold disk, break the spell, and find out what he's up to.

If you grab the disk and confront Phaino, turn to page 20.

If you wake Nina and run, turn to page 52.

"I don't know what you're talking about," Nina says bravely.

"Never mind, my dear lying mortal," says Carmilla. "We will know soon enough. The old woman is sure to tell us where she has hidden the jewel. We can be most . . . persuasive." Then she's gone like smoke.

"We have to follow them," says Nina. "We've got to save my aunt."

"Wait! Listen!" cries Phaino. "The only hope for Mrs. West—or for any of us—is to follow my plan. My trap *will* capture the vampires. I'm sure of it."

*If you decide to follow Zoltan and Carmilla,
turn to page 106.*

*If you decide to follow Phaino's plan,
turn to page 36.*

You call Nina's name one last time, then sadly turn to follow Nanosh and Andrew toward the vampires' lair. When the fog is far behind you, you round a bend . . . and there it is, a dark and evil-looking ruin silhouetted against the evening sky. The ramparts and battlements are crumbling, and only one of the original towers remains standing.

When you reach the castle, you find the gate closed and locked. Andrew tugs on the rusty bell chain, but all you hear is laughter. You look more closely at the run-down wall. It's full of chinks and cracks, and you think you might be able to climb it.

"If I can get over the wall and open the gate from the inside, we can attack the vampires now," you say.

"Too risky," says Nanosh.

"Better to wait till morning, when the vampires must rest," says Andrew.

They're probably right, but you're tired of waiting.

If you take their advice and wait, turn to page 90.

If you climb the wall when Andrew and Nanosh are asleep, turn to page 95.

You leap to Nina's aid. Carmilla is dazed. Never before has anyone attacked her so ferociously. But dazed isn't enough. Can a vampire be knocked unconscious, you wonder. There's only one way to find out. You pick up one of Phaino's heavy laser projectors—only to find yourself snatched away from the countess. Zoltan's iron fingers grab you by the neck, lift you into the air, and shake you till you drop the projector.

"Filthy piglets," hisses the countess.

"And the little she pig is attempting to escape," adds the count. "Hold onto this one, my dear, while I attend to the other."

While the count was busy with you, Nina ducked away. And now she is deep within the maze of old baggage and boxes that fill most of the car. She moves swiftly and easily, but the count is too large to follow her path. He has to plow through the jumble, moving crates and cartons aside. For an instant you worry that Nina is deserting you, but then you realize she's headed for the painting.

What is Phaino doing, you wonder. Why doesn't he try to spring his trap? But Phaino isn't doing anything. He is paralyzed with fear. If the painting truly can help, you think, now is certainly the time for it.

Turn to page 10.

It's so cold and drafty in the corridor of the old passenger car, you and Nina put on your quilted goose-down jackets, and the professor dons his long overcoat. He is extremely careful and thorough in his search for clues. On hands and knees he examines every speck of lint, each scrap of paper. He reminds you a little of Sherlock Holmes. But the trouble is, after what seems like hours, he still hasn't found a useful clue.

As time passes, Nina grows more and more impatient. Finally she's had it. "All this busywork is a waste of time," she says angrily, her hands on her hips. "I'm going to search somewhere else." She strides quickly to the end of the corridor and opens the door that leads back to Count Zoltan's car.

"Nina, the conductor said—" you begin, but Nina interrupts with a shout.

"Come here," she cries triumphantly. "Come see what I've found." When you and the professor reach her, she waves a white lace hankie in your faces. "My aunt's," she says, pointing to a large *W* embroidered in one corner. "She *must* be in the last car."

"There's only one way to find out," you say, twisting the large brass doorknob.

The door is locked.

*If you try to force the door open,
turn to page 58.*

*If you knock on the door,
turn to page 104.*

When you open the door, the wind and snow hit you like razors. You grab a rung of the ladder and start to climb, wishing you had gloves. The only thing to do is keep going and try not to think about the freezing metal. Cautiously, you raise your head over the edge of the roof and look around. Toward the rear of the train you see the eerie glow of the jewel. You clamber up onto the roof; then you lean down to lend Nina and the professor a hand.

The three of you are practically on hands and knees as you carefully work your way toward the rear of the swaying train. But the man you're following—if it *is* a man—walks as if he's sauntering along a country lane in June.

The train makes a hard lurch, and you teeter dangerously to one side. But Nina catches you just in time.

Finally the man pauses somewhere on the roof of the last car—the one the conductor told you about: Count Zoltan's private car. Suddenly a blaze of light shines out of the rooftop. It's a trap door. Swiftly the man descends, and the door closes.

A few moments later, the three of you are on the count's car. You look around and discover that there are *two* trap doors: one near the front, and one, which the man used, near the rear. At the very end of the car, there's a ladder that goes down to an observation platform.

You all agree it's too risky to follow the man through the rear trap door. But the observation platform probably has a door to the room he has just entered. Or you could try an indirect approach and use the trap door at the front of the car.

If you try the front trap door, turn to page 11.

If you use the ladder, turn to page 97.

"Nina! Nina! Get hold of yourself," Phaino shouts as you hit Nina with a diving tackle, knocking her away from Carmilla. The countess sits up. Though she still looks startled by Nina's sudden attack, she's also terribly angry. She raises her arm to strike a ferocious blow, but you and Nina scramble away on your hands and knees. When you look back, the count is standing over his wife, helping her to her feet.

"Ahh, my poor Carmilla," he says lovingly. "You've taken a wicked fall. I hope you are not hurt."

"Kill the little witch," Carmilla hisses, pointing her long thin hand at Nina.

Turn to page 113.

Bela leads in Mrs. West. She is pale and glassy-eyed, and she walks like someone working hard not to stumble and fall.

"Aunt, what is the matter," Nina cries, rushing to her side.

"I . . . am . . . fine," says Mrs. West.

Nina turns on the count. "What have you done to her?" she demands.

"Please, please, do not be alarmed," says the count. "The lady has suffered something of an upset. But soon she'll be back in top form, I promise. We wish only the best for her. After all, she is the one who made it possible for us to retrieve our long-lost property: the painting"—he gestures toward the box—"and the Blood-stone"—he points to the necklace. "The fabulous jewel that renders the painting harmless to us."

As if it has heard its name, the Bloodstone begins to blaze. The light from it is brilliant and red as blood. You find that you can't take your eyes from it. And you can't move.

"Ahh," says Carmilla. "Now you begin to understand the jewel's power. And why it makes life so much more bearable for us."

"And as for you," says the count, "we will let you off the train at a pleasant little village—a portion of our estates. There you will meet some old friends of ours."

Two hours later, the train stops, and Count Zoltan conducts you and Nina, the professor and Mrs. West into a village. He rings a bell set on a post in the village square.

Turn to page 57.

Noiselessly you twist the latch of the first door. The room, you discover, is Countess Carmilla's bedroom. But where her bed should be, there's a coffin!

Expensive looking clothes are scattered across the floor. Out of curiosity, you open the closet door—and discover Mrs. West. She's tied to a chair and gagged.

The three of you swiftly undo her bindings, and Mrs. West springs up, stamping her foot like a child having a tantrum.

Turn to page 96.

"I want to go home!" Nina says at once. "And I want my aunt with us. Can you send her, too?"

"Probably," says Bela. "Any other ideas?"

"Maybe you should send us all to my uncle Andrew," you suggest. "What do you think, Professor?"

"I think this is a farce," he says with a scowl. "Just get it over with so that we can go about our business."

"Well, make up your minds," says Bela.

If you say, "Send us to Uncle Andrew," turn to page 19.

If you say, "Send us home," turn to page 43.

You and Nina are almost exhausted, but you stumble on.

"Faster, faster," Nanosh shouts. "Don't stop, whatever you do. Sing! *Sing!*"

The ring of people closes in on the fire—and so do the vampires above you. When you are all nearly touching the flames, the painting suddenly ignites. Flames hurtle upward and engulf the vampires. There are twin explosions, and you all fall unconscious.

In the morning you and Nina are the last to wake up. And there is Uncle Andrew, who has just arrived. A Gypsy messenger reached him about the time you set out for the vampires' lair. With a broad smile, Andrew helps you up and points to the castle. Walking unsteadily through the gate is Mrs. West! Nanosh hurries off to lend her a hand, while the rest of the Gypsies begin to pack up.

"It's a shame you didn't take photos last night," Andrew says, "but I suspect that with you and the others as witnesses, and with the evidence we'll find in the castle itself, there will be no possible doubt about the existence of vampires."

He raises his arms to catch everyone's attention and in a loud, hearty voice announces, "You have all done simply wonderfully. Grand work! Grand, grand work!"

The End

You search the castle for Mrs. West and find her lying on a stone slab. The destruction of the vampires seems to have released her from a trance, and soon she's as strong as ever—and complaining.

"Andrew, you old toad," she says. "What took you so long? Where is my niece? And my jewel? And my painting?"

Andrew begins to explain about losing Nina in the fog, when suddenly there's no need. Nina herself is standing in the doorway. She dashes over and gives her aunt a big hug. Then she describes her escape.

"I managed to climb a tree before the wolves could find me," she says. "When they gave up and the fog lifted, I climbed down and found my horse. I set off after you right away, but I seem to have missed all the excitement." She pretends to pout, but she can't help laughing.

Meanwhile, Andrew has retrieved his camera from the pack of supplies. "Hold it right there, Nina; the rest of you, too," he says. "I want some pictures for my records."

There's a flash. Then another flash. Then another.

Andrew doesn't have to remind anyone to smile. You've never felt happier.

The End

"Thanks very much," you say, "but we really must find Nina's aunt, Mrs. West. She disappeared about an hour ago, and even though we've searched the train, we can't find her."

"Disappeared?" says the count. "Hardly. She has, in fact, been visiting with us. We have found her . . . mmm . . . most pleasant. I believe she is resting in my dear wife's bedroom. Would you like to say hello to her?"

"We sure would," Nina says eagerly.

"Then you shall, immediately," replies the count. "Bela, take them to Mrs. West."

Grumbling loudly, Bela yanks open the door and pushes you into the corridor. But the moment the parlor door is safely shut his manner changes. "Run," he whispers urgently. "Don't lose a second! Run to the painting. The count and countess are vampires. They will kill you unless you get to the painting first. It's your only chance—and my only hope of escaping eternal bondage. I'll try to delay them, but hurry . . . hurry!"

Turn to page 107.

"Does anyone have a suggestion?" you ask.

"Maybe the professor and my aunt can create a diversion to draw the vampires away," says Nina. "Meanwhile, you and I can sneak over the roof to the observation platform and into the room where the painting is being kept. If they can keep the vampires busy long enough, we can recover the painting—and turn it against them."

"That sounds terribly dangerous," says Mrs. West. "I suggest we all wait here until morning. You can bind me again—loosely, mind you— and then hide behind the drapes. When the vampires return to their coffins at daylight, we can recover the painting."

The professor stands aside and says nothing, a deep scowl on his face. Obviously he has his own ideas, but he chooses not to reveal them. So it's up to you to decide which plan to follow.

If you think it's better to try stealing the painting now, turn to page 16.

If you think it's better to wait till morning, turn to page 42.

Single file, the four of you descend into the crypt. The arched stone ceiling is so low that Uncle Andrew has to bend over to walk, and there is no real floor. Instead there's a swampy mixture of mud and filth.

The four of you walk on and on. Just as you're about to give up hope, you come upon them: not only the two vampires, sleeping in their coffins, but Mrs. West as well, laid out on a stone slab.

Nina touches her aunt's face. "Oh, no!" she sobs. "She's dead!"

Turn to page 44.

The painting snarls.

You remember Luluvo's Star and raise the crystal high over your head with both hands. The Bloodstone dims! The Star has drained its powers.

The painting snarls again, and a bright golden serpent of light surges out of it. The serpent coils and then rockets toward the red eyes above. The vampires can do nothing to evade the terrible serpent. It consumes them in a brilliant ball of fire.

Later you find Mrs. West in one of the crypt rooms. She is sitting up on a stone slab, rubbing the sleep out of her eyes. Before long the Gypsies join you, and the next morning Andrew arrives— too late, he greatly regrets, to take part in the adventures. Still, he has never looked happier. At last he has the proof he's been seeking.

The End

Reluctantly, Nina and Mrs. West step forward and go to work releasing the secret locks that protect the painting. The count and countess hover over them, watching every move they make.

Meanwhile, your mind is working like mad on a way to escape.

One possibility is starting a fire. The parlor is lit by candles and oil lamps. If you moved really fast, while the vampires' attention was focused on the painting, you just might be able to spill enough oil to start a good-size blaze. In the confusion that followed, the four of you would have a chance of escaping.

Another possibility is snatching the jewel. If you could get rid of the Bloodstone, the painting would regain its powers. Nina is close enough to Carmilla to grab the necklace. If she threw it to you, you could toss it out the window you broke to get into this place. But you'll need a signal—some code word—that only Nina will recognize. A word that suggests stealing jewels.

The box begins to open. You have to decide.

If you try to start a fire, turn to page 14.

If you think you can come up with a code word, turn to page 92.

86

"But if they're vampires, we can't leave my aunt to them," says Nina.

"We can do nothing for your aunt here," says Nanosh. "We do not know how to use the painting's powers—only Andrew and the Old Ones have that knowledge."

"The Old Ones?" you say.

"They are the spirits who guide us," explains Nanosh. "They speak through Lyuba, our wise woman. If you carry the painting to our camp, we can consult them in safety. Your other choice is to try to contact your uncle at the next station, to ask for his advice. Once we know how to use the painting, we can follow the vampires to their castle. Until then we can only hope that Mrs. West is still alive."

If you decide to try to contact Uncle Andrew, turn to page 22.

If you decide to take the painting to the Gypsy camp, turn to page 64.

The two of you turn and dash through the rear door and out onto the observation platform. There's a ladder to the roof. You clamber up, hoping to make your way along the top of the swaying train to the passenger car ahead.

The train slowly climbs a steep grade. The snowstorm has become a blizzard, and the wind that hits you is fierce and bitter. You grab what handholds you can as you half run, half crawl toward safety. Trap doors swing open. Hands stretch out to snatch at you. But somehow you slip around them. And now, behind you, in spite of the roar of the wind, you hear the heavy, steady pounding of the vampire's feet.

"We'll never make it," you shout to Nina. "Our only chance is to jump for it."

The two of you leap blindly into the dark . . . and land in a soft snowbank, shaken but safe.

The blizzard is bad, but the train was worse, and you're not sorry to hear it rumble away. You're lucky the count decided not to jump after you, and your luck continues to hold. In the distance you can see a warm yellow light.

Soon you and Nina find yourselves in a cozy cabin belonging to a woodsman and his wife, who gladly put you up for the night. The next morning you follow the railroad tracks to town, where you call Uncle Andrew. Maybe he'll be able to find Mrs. West. You certainly hope so.

The End

The car just ahead is a coal car, and you and Nina scramble over it. Your mind is so fixed on escape, you don't even mind the lash of the bitterly cold wind and snow. Finally you reach the cab of the engine.

"Hey!" you call out. "Help! There are vampires back there."

The engineer doesn't even turn around. He stares straight ahead, as if he's in a trance, both hands gripping the throttle.

The train is climbing a steep mountain grade, and the fireman shovels coal furiously to keep up the steam pressure. He doesn't look up or speak. When you're nearly at the top of the grade, there's a sudden sharp lurch, and the engine surges forward. Oh, no! The vampires have uncoupled the train. The cars are rolling backward down the mountain, but—freed of their weight—the engine hurtles on.

"Stop! Stop!" you yell, trying to pull the engineer's hands from the throttle. But his grip doesn't loosen, and the fireman keeps shoveling coal like a machine.

Faster and faster the engine races along the tracks. The railroad bed has been cut into a narrow ledge, and below the ledge there's a terrifying sheer drop. The engine strains to leave the track. It wants to take off like a plane.

And now it does take off. It springs from the track, arcs through the air, and plunges down . . . down . . . down. . . .

The End

The three of you build a fire and cook a hearty meal of sausages, beans, and pan-baked bread. You volunteer to take the first watch while the others sleep. You're not worried about staying awake; at this point it seems safer than closing your eyes!

Around eleven o'clock you hear feet slapping on stones, pebbles clicking, and a snuffling noise, like a dog worrying a bone.

Go on to the next page.

Silently you remove a flashlight from the pack of supplies Andrew brought along. Then you creep toward the sounds. When you judge you're close enough, you switch on the light. The beam sweeps past a pile of broken stones and debris—and catches a little man, bent, misshapen, and incredibly ugly.

For a moment you stare at one another. Then he scuttles away, turns a corner, and disappears. If you follow him, you might find another way into the castle. Then again, you might find yourself in a trap.

If you return to the campsite, turn to page 6.

If you go after the little man, turn to page 50.

You have it. You'll base your code on *The Pink Panther,* the Inspector Clouseau movie about the fabulous pink diamond that's stolen again and again.

As Nina and her aunt open the box, the vampires bend closer to them, almost shivering with anticipation. Their eyes are glued to Nina as she lifts up the painting and leans it against the wall. It's a portrait of Zoltan and Carmilla, done many hundreds of years before. They step back a pace to admire themselves.

Softly you begin to whistle the theme from *The Pink Panther,* and you back away from the painting . . . carefully . . . moving toward the broken window.

"What's that annoying tune, mortal?" Carmilla demands, turning to stare at you.

You freeze. "Ah, it's just a song from a movie about a funny man who catches, um"—you clear your throat—"a jewel thief."

"Ugly stuff," she says, turning back to the painting. "I despise your music."

"Oh, gee, I'm sorry," you stammer. "I didn't mean to bother you. I was only trying to—you know—cheer myself up. You remember *The Pink Panther*, don't you, Nina?"

Nina stares at you, her brow furrowed.

Oh, no! She hasn't caught on.

Turn to page 59.

CRASH!

You open your eyes . . . and find yourself back in your train compartment. What's happening? Have you been dreaming? Nina is next to you, curled up and fast asleep. Across from you is Mrs. West, also asleep. On the floor is the carved wooden box that guards the painting Nina is bringing to your uncle Andrew. The painting that . . . that . . .

How did it get here? How did *you* get here?

You glance at Mrs. West's neck. Yes, she is wearing the red jewel. Why shouldn't she be, you ask yourself. Yet somehow the jewel disturbs you. You feel it's not good, though you can't say why.

Then you remember the incredible wind and the vampires flying after you. Were you really there? Were *they*? Are they still there? Could the painting have trapped Zoltan and Carmilla in the windy spaces and then returned you and Nina to your own world? You certainly hope so.

Nina and her aunt wake up, and for a long time the three of you stare at one another wordlessly. You all avoid asking the questions in your minds. Best not to ask them . . . best to leave them buried . . . best to believe it was all nothing but a dream.

The End

At first the climbing is easy. The wall is full of large cracks and ledges. But higher up, the going gets rougher and riskier. The ledges break when you step on them. The stones crumble in your hands. Still you struggle upward, higher and higher.

You are near the end of your climb. Your right hand reaches over the top of the wall . . . and something bites it! Flames seem to be raging up your arm. There's another bite. And another. Each one makes the pain worse, and you're not sure you can hold on. With great effort you lift your head up over the wall and see monstrous, hairy black spiders—thousands of them. They leap toward you.

You let go of the wall. For you it's

The End

"Well," says Mrs. West, stamping her other foot. "Now my blood is moving again—although I must say that I'm probably lucky to have blood at all. I have just had a *most* disagreeable experience, one I would not soon care to repeat. So I am very glad to see you two." Then she turns to the professor. "And who, pray tell, are you? she asks.

"I am Professor Emile Hartz," he replies. "I am an investigator into the unexplained."

"Uncle Andrew asked him to join the vampire expedition," you say.

"You mean the wild goose chase," the professor sneers.

"Ha! Stop right there," Mrs. West says in a voice that could break bricks. "There are two vampires on this very train. In this very car. They captured me in the baggage car and brought me here. After they tied me up, they had the nerve to introduce themselves and brag about their wicked deeds. Can you imagine!"

"Frankly, madam, I cannot," says Professor Hartz. But Mrs. West ignores him and goes on with her story.

"Their names are Count Zoltan and Countess Carmilla. During the day, she sleeps there," she says, pointing to the coffin. "They travel in this car from town to town, stopping for a few days at a time until"—her voice drops chillingly—"they have taken their fill of blood. Then they move on, before the townspeople realize what has befallen them."

Turn to page 109.

Nina and Professor Hartz follow you down the ladder to the observation platform. You were right. There is a door leading into Zoltan's car. The three of you peer through one of the windows that flank it and see an elegant old-fashioned parlor. Across the room is the wooden box that holds the painting. And next to it stand a man and woman dressed in evening clothes. He is the one you followed across the roof of the car; she has on Mrs. West's jewel. Both of them are staring straight at you with smiles cold and nasty enough to freeze hydrogen.

The man glides across the room and opens the door. "May we join you on *our* balcony?" he says pointedly. "I hope that the journey across the roof was not too trying for you mortals. I must confess I find it exhilarating. But I am forgetting my manners. My name, if you do not yet know it, is Zoltan. The lady is my wife, Carmilla."

Carmilla inclines her head. "I'm sure these people would like to see Mrs. West," she says.

"Yes, such a delectable lady," says Zoltan. Then he sweeps around imperiously. "Bela! Bela!" he shouts. "Where have you gone, you lazy good-for-nothing?"

"The last time I saw him he was in his closet, roasting moths in a candle flame," says Carmilla.

"*Roasting moths!*" the professor repeats.

"You don't think he'd eat them raw?" Carmilla asks in a shocked voice.

The ugliest man you've ever seen slinks into the parlor.

Turn to page 110.

You peek through the door into a luxurious but old-fashioned parlor. It is lit by candles and oil lamps, and in the far corner sits a pot-bellied stove with a roaring fire inside. The box that holds the painting has been placed against the far wall. The Bloodstone lies on a table next to it. No one is in the room. The diversion must have worked!

You try the door, but it's locked. There's a tall window on either side of it. With your elbow you tap at the corner of the window nearest the doorknob. Not hard enough. You tap harder, and a piece of the glass breaks. You reach through the opening and unlock the door. As you and Nina tiptoe into the room, a short, repulsive little man enters it from the opposite side. He sees you and stops dead in his tracks.

In another second, he'll shout an alarm.

Turn to page 45.

Lyuba flings the emerald stone into the depths of the flames. Thunder booms. Huge, bright billows of green smoke swell from the fire and swallow her. Finally the smoke drifts away, and you can see that she is now holding an odd-shaped crystal about three or four inches across.

"This is the message of the stone," she says in a grave voice. "You have been appointed leader of those who will combat the vampires. This places

Go on to the next page.

you in terrible peril, for Countess Carmilla now wears the Bloodstone, the jewel they took from Mrs. West. It makes them nearly invulnerable by draining the great powers of the painting.

"However, the Old Ones will not send you against Zoltan and Carmilla unshielded. They are giving you this crystal, called Luluvo's Star. Luluvo was our greatest king and a terrible enemy of vampires. It is our hope that his crystal star will protect you against the blood light of the jewel and will allow the powers of the painting to overcome the vampires."

The next morning you and Nina, Nanosh, and several other Gypsies set off on horseback for the vampires' lair. Toward evening, when the castle is in sight, Nanosh turns to you and gestures toward a tall, rocky spire. "That high pinnacle is one of our most sacred places," he says. "It is called Gypsy's Needle. We could climb to its top and wait there for the painting to attract the count and countess. Now that they have the Bloodstone, they may be overconfident and try to attack us on our own ground. However, if Mrs. West is still alive, it might be better if we entered the castle immediately. Both ways are filled with peril, but the choice is yours. You are the leader."

If you go on to the vampires' castle, turn to page 32.

If you wait at the top of Gypsy's Needle, turn to page 116.

Luckily, Nina's horse is not far off, and you find the medical supplies in her pack. Gently and carefully you clean and bandage her wound. Then you set off after Nanosh and Andrew. For Nina's sake you are forced to travel slowly, but you do catch up to them at nightfall.

Early the next morning you ride to the vampires' lair. The castle is in ruins, except for one tall tower. But Andrew says, "If I know my vampires, that pile is not what it appears to be. There will be miles of tunnels and dozens of rooms hidden beneath the ruins. And somewhere there is a crypt where the vampires sleep during the day."

"Look," says Nanosh, "the gate is open."

"Then let's unpack the painting and go in," says Andrew.

Inside the gate you find a courtyard, and across the courtyard there's a set of wide stone steps that curve up to a door in the tower. Near the foot of the staircase is another doorway, which Andrew says he thinks leads to the crypt.

"It seems we have two choices," says Andrew. "We can split up, or we can all go down into the crypt. Nanosh and I *must* take the painting and try to destroy the vampires. But if you wish, you and Nina can search the tower for Mrs. West."

*If you want to look for Mrs. West,
turn to page 62.*

*If you want to go with Uncle Andrew and
Nanosh, turn to page 83.*

A tall, elegant man in evening clothes appears. He yanks the bent little man roughly aside and bows graciously. "Please come in," he says. "I am Zoltan. Forgive my oaf of a servant, Bela. Nothing I do to him seems to make him hospitable."

The count's car is luxurious—full of gleaming wood, soft leather, and polished brass—but it is also very old-fashioned. He leads you down a long corridor to a parlor lit by candles and oil lamps.

"My lovely wife, Carmilla," Zoltan says, gesturing toward a beautiful woman reclining on a sofa. She is so still that until that moment you hadn't even noticed her.

"Bela, bring these young people refreshments," Zoltan orders.

Nina tries to ask about her aunt, but the count interrupts. "In a moment we will talk, but first do us the honor of enjoying a light repast."

In a moment Bela arrives with a serving cart. On it are bowls of candy and platters of cookies, cakes, and pastries, pitchers of fruit punch and pots of hot chocolate. Everything looks delicious.

Although you're anxious to keep searching for Mrs. West, you find your mouth watering and suddenly realize you haven't eaten for hours.

The countess seems to come to life. "Please take what you like," she says sweetly, but you notice a strange look in her eyes.

If you accept her invitation, turn to page 61.

If you decline, turn to page 81.

Before long, a bent, twisted, little man opens
the door a crack. He is ugly beyond description,
and his eyes look flat and dead.

"I am Professor Emile Hartz," says the professor. "My companions and I are searching for an

elderly lady whose name is West. Perhaps you have seen her."

"I am Bela," says the little man in a voice that grates like ungreased hinges. "Come in." He opens the door a little wider.

Zoltan's car looks ancient, but it has been treated well. The polished wooden walls gleam, the brass fixtures are shiny, and the place is even warm—quite a change from the car you just left behind.

Bela leads you down a corridor past three doors and through a fourth door into a parlor. It is lit by oil lamps and candles, and there is an old-fashioned wood stove in one corner. Not far from that stands a large wooden box with strange carvings all over it. A glance at Nina confirms what you suspected: the painting is in that box.

A handsome man and a beautiful woman are seated together on a sofa. Mrs. West's jewel hangs from the woman's neck.

"Good evening," the man says, rising. "I am Count Zoltan, and this is my lovely wife, Carmilla. What a delight to receive visitors on such a boring night."

The three of you introduce yourselves, and the professor explains your purpose in coming.

"Yes, of course your Mrs. West has been with us," says the count. "We have had a very pleasant time with her indeed." He raises his arm. "Bela," he orders, "you will bring the lady."

Turn to page 75.

Zoltan lopes toward the rear of the train, with Mrs. West draped across his shoulders like a stole. At the entrance to his private car, he turns and raises his arm. "Fools! To pursue *me!*" he cries.

Darkness closes down on you, and there's an evil, suffocating stench. You feel yourself gliding . . . as if you're in a dream. Where am I, you wonder.

You wake. You're in a strange room with a vaulted stone ceiling. You look about and discover that Nina, Mrs. West, and Phaino are nearby. But how they've changed! Their eyes glow like rubies. Their fingernails have grown long and sharp, like knives. And their teeth have become narrow and pointed, like fangs.

You examine your own hands. Your nails are like theirs! And your teeth. . . .

"I am thirsty," says Mrs. West. "I will go to drink." She rises and shuffles off toward an ancient stone staircase.

"I am, too," Nina says, and she rises and follows her aunt.

Then you and Phaino rise and shuffle to the stairs.

All four of you file out of the castle into the night. Somewhere in the valley below—or in the next valley, perhaps—you will find living people. And they will begin to satisfy *this* night's thirst.

The End

You and Nina race through the train. When you reach the baggage car, you hear feet pounding behind you. But you don't dare look back.

Once inside, a strange force lifts Nina off her feet and carries her over to an intricately carved wooden box. Her hands dart over its surface, releasing hidden latches and opening invisible locks.

In a few seconds the box is open, and Nina snatches the painting from its resting place. At that moment the door is flung open, and Zoltan and Carmilla bound inside.

When they catch sight of the painting, they let out an incredible moan of pain. "Ahhhhh," they cry. "Too late . . . too late! Lost . . . we are lost!"

Whips of flame lash out of the painting and twine around the vampires. Their bodies shrink and curl like paper in a hot fire. And then Zoltan and Carmilla are nothing but ashes.

You and Nina stare at one another, speechless. What you've just seen is too incredible for words. But you know you'll have a lot to say when you see Uncle Andrew.

The End

"What's going on?" you yell. "What is this stuff?"

"We call it the vampire fog," says Nanosh. "It appears just like that"—he snaps his fingers—"and people can get lost in it for days. I'm afraid we may not find Nina."

Keeping close together, you try to retrace your way. But the fog is so thick, you can barely see your horses' heads in front of you. When you call out Nina's name, the fog swallows your voices. You keep searching, but there is no trace of her.

Finally Andrew calls a halt. "I don't think we'll find her now," he says, "and if we're not careful, we'll get lost, too. It's vitally important that we take the painting to the vampires' castle. We can return for Nina after the fog lifts."

"But what about the wolves?" you say. "Nina's on foot!"

"The wolves will be practically helpless in this fog," says Nanosh. "If she climbs a tree, she has a good chance of escaping them."

"I'll understand if you want to stay and search for Nina," says Andrew. "But if you're coming with us, you must come now."

If you stay to look for Nina, turn to page 54.

*If you go with Andrew and Nanosh,
turn to page 69.*

"What shall we do?" asks Nina.

"Is the painting safe?" asks Mrs. West.

"No, they have it," you reply, "and the jewel, too."

"Oh, drat," says Mrs. West. "That certainly complicates things. I hid the jewel in a jumble of crates right before they caught me. But they did unspeakable things to me, and I was forced to tell them the hiding place. I hoped they wouldn't find the painting."

"Why do they want the painting and the jewel in the first place?" asks Nina.

"From what I've pieced together, they *need* the jewel, which they call the Bloodstone," answers Mrs. West. "By itself, the painting can do them terrible harm. But if they have it *and* the Bloodstone, they can't be hurt. The Bloodstone neutralizes the painting."

"So Uncle Andrew was right," you say. "The painting and the jewel *do* have awesome powers."

"Yes," says Mrs. West. "And we must get them back, or the vampires will be invulnerable."

Turn to page 82.

The man is small and stocky, and his body is bent like a banana. There's a frightened expression on his swollen, puffy face. When he opens the door, the count aims a vicious kick in his direction. But the little man dodges it nimbly. He may look awkward, but he's quick!

"Bela, bring in Mrs. West," the count commands.

Shortly after, Bela returns to the platform with Nina's aunt. Although she looks a bit dazed, she seems otherwise all right. Zoltan clasps one of her hands in both of his. "I must thank you again, dear lady, for the painting and the jewel—the fabulous Bloodstone."

"Oh, indeed yes," Carmilla says brightly. "We simply *adore* the Bloodstone. In fact, we can't live without it!"

"But now we must bid you farewell," says Zoltan. "We require your presence no longer."

The next thing you know, the floor has dropped away, and you, Nina, Mrs. West, and the professor are flat on your backs on the snowy tracks. You look after the disappearing train and see Zoltan and Carmilla, still standing there and waving, just as though there were a real floor beneath them.

So there you are, in the middle of a mountain wilderness in a blizzard. But at least you're alive and away from the vampires. And maybe Andrew will be able to come up with a new scheme for trapping the count and his wife.

The End

You grab Nina's arm. "I don't believe it," you tell her.

"Neither do I," she says. "I never thought I'd walk into my own room *here!*"

"*Your* room?" you say. "But this is *my* room!"

Just then Mrs. West and Uncle Andrew walk through the door. "Hello, my dears," they say together.

The painting makes a growling noise, breaks free of Nina, and lunges at them.

"Those guys are fakes!" you shout.

Nina stumbles after the painting, and as you rush to help her, the fake Andrew and Mrs. West change into bats and fly down the tunnel—which has suddenly reappeared. Nina manages to grab the painting, but it drags her along as it pursues the bats.

"Follow! Follow!" a voice shouts in your mind. "Those bats are vampires. They must be destroyed."

Down the tunnel you race, chasing Nina chasing the vampires. At least you don't have to worry about torches; the painting lights the way. At last you find yourselves in a vast, steamy cavern. Millions of bats fill the air, but only two of them have eyes like glowing coals. And only one of those two wears the Bloodstone. It glows like the vampires' eyes, filling you with dread.

Turn to page 84.

"Now," Phaino whispers and throws the main switch. At once the lasers blaze with brilliant red, green, and blue light.

Carmilla grins. Hand in hand, she and Zoltan glide right into the center of the vampire trap—and stop in their tracks. The laser beams are so bright they appear solid. They seem to weave a net around the count and countess.

"You see!" Phaino cries joyfully. "It works! It works! You can see them in the mirrors. For the first time in history, a vampire's reflection has been caught in a mirror."

He's right. The vampires' reflections *are* caught in the mirrors. Then Zoltan and Carmilla laugh their horrible, deathly laughs. And move.

"This is sooo nice," the countess exclaims.

"Yes, my love," says the count. "I'm so very glad you invited me to come along."

They *like* it! They enjoy the vampire trap! They kick up their heels and begin to dance a tango in the laser beams.

"It's not working," you scream at Phaino. You begin to back away from the trap. Maybe you and Nina can still escape.

"Stay," Phaino says. "It *will* work, I promise. Just a little more power." He twists a black knob on the control panel.

If you stay, turn to page 24.

If you try to escape, turn to page 26.

You and Nina sneak back to the box with the weird carvings. A strange, pulsing halo of light now surrounds it. The box itself shimmers, and the wood no longer looks quite real . . . . or quite solid.

Nina reaches out to touch the box—and her hand passes through its surface, as though it were an open window. Startled, she snatches her hand back and stares at it in disbelief. A few moments later she says, "You won't believe this, but the painting says it has used its powers to become a gateway into another space. It wants us to pass through."

Go on to the next page.

You're about to say thanks but no thanks when you glance in the vampires' direction. They have stopped dancing. Zoltan is staring at you with the greedy, triumphant look of a cat about to pounce on a sparrow. And then, once more, the two vampires turn into bats and launch themselves in your direction. So you change your mind. "What have we got to lose?" you tell Nina as you move toward the shimmering box.

Suddenly a howling, keening wind bursts upon you, a wind louder than the wildest hurricane. And the next thing you know, it picks you and Nina up and hurls you both through the gateway into a dark, frightening void.

It seems, then, that you are falling. But there's no way to be sure, because you can't see anything. Nor can you hear anything above the hurricane roar. All you feel is the wind carrying you along, and the pressure of someone's hand grasping yours. Is it Nina's hand? You hope so.

After a time, the air around you grows brighter, and you begin to make out Nina's welcome face. It *is* her hand you're holding. But then your heart sinks. Not far behind you are two huge bats— Zoltan and Carmilla—trying mightily to catch up to you.

They come closer and closer. Their dagger-sharp fangs gleam. Their ruby lips are moist and quivering. Their claws stretch out for you. . . .

Turn to page 93.

You climb to the Needle's summit and watch the sun set behind Zoltan's crumbling, ruined castle. Then the Gypsies build a large bonfire while Nina.removes the painting from its box and you take Luluvo's Star from your backpack. Nanosh sets up the painting so that it faces the vampires' castle and yet receives the full light of the fire. Then, with his dagger, he draws an eye in the dirt between the painting and the fire, and you place the crystal in the eye's pupil.

Joining hands, everyone makes a ring around the fire. "Now we are ready for them," Nanosh says with grim determination. "But remember! The fire must not go out. If it dies, we are lost."

Wolves howl. Flocks of screaming bats whirl and dive within inches of your heads. But they don't attack. Then the wind picks up and a gusting, misty rain threatens the fire. But you and the Gypsies take turns adding log after log to the blaze, and the fire never dims.

At midnight Nanosh cries, "Everyone on his feet. Now we dance and sing!" And around the blazing bonfire you go, dancing and singing at the top of your lungs.

The wolves howl again, and then you see two monster bats flying above you. The vampires! They are circling the fire, drawn to it like comets to the sun. Around one of the bat's necks is the Bloodstone. Its terrible crimson glow falls on you like a lead shroud and drains you of your energy.

Turn to page 79.

You hear the sound of large wings flapping, and two giant bats appear. They alight on the floor nearby and change into a man and woman dressed in evening clothes and capes. The man seizes Mrs. West and tosses her like a sack over his shoulder. Mrs. West screams and kicks, but he ignores her.

"Please excuse my lack of manners," the man says. "Usually I do not appear so unexpectedly before . . . new friends. However, this lady has hidden our property, the Bloodstone, and I must see that she restores it to us." He turns to leave, then turns back again. "Ah, yes. Doubtless, you wish to know our names. I am Count Zoltan, and she is my wife, Countess Carmilla." Then he bounds away with Mrs. West.

Carmilla remains behind. Her face is so twisted with rage it looks like a nest of snakes. "The Bloodstone!" she shrieks. It's a cry that would freeze birds in flight. "Where is it? Where did the old woman hide it? We must have it. *Now!*"

Turn to page 67.

A cry of pain comes from the wooden box that holds the painting. And that makes the vampires dance with even greater energy.

"Why didn't you provide us with music?" Zoltan asks. "Aren't we friends?"

"Mmmm," says Carmilla. "Even without it, I'm having a perfectly marvelous time. The lasers feel like a nice freezing bath."

The painting cries again, a cry of infinite loss. In answer, a choking sob comes from deep within Nina's throat. But, like you, she cannot speak or move.

The single light bulb in the baggage car shatters. The lasers fail. But the darkness lasts only seconds. Then there's a new light . . . a blood red glow that comes from beneath a pile of cartons. The glow pulses and throbs as though a beating heart drives it.

"Ahh, yes," says Zoltan, raising his cape high over his head. "So that's where the old woman hid our jewel, our precious Bloodstone. It has been returned to us at last after these many centuries. For this priceless gift we will give you mortals a gift in return. We will allow you to join the ranks of the undead."

The End

ABOUT THE AUTHOR

TONY KOLTZ was born and grew up in Dallas, Texas, and was educated by the Jesuits and at Columbia University. He was for many years associate editor of the literary magazine *The American Review* and a senior editor at Bantam Books. He is married and has two boys, David and Jonathan. In addition to *Vampire Express,* Mr. Koltz is the author of Choose Your Own Adventure #59, *Terror Island.*

ABOUT THE ILLUSTRATOR

DOUG JAMIESON, illustrator, teacher, and writer, lives in New York City with his wife, Pat, and their children, Leslie and Kris. A graduate of the School of Visual Arts, Doug has been illustrating for magazines, books, and children's publications since the late '60s. He recently co-authored and illustrated *What's GNU?* and has illustrated *Mice Are Rather Nice, Spoonbread and Strawberry Wine, The Christmas Almanack, The Pop-Up Book of the American Revolution,* and *Oops!* Doug teaches illustration and drawing at the School of Visual Arts. He is currently writing and illustrating a book on anatomy based on his classroom lectures.

CHOOSE YOUR OWN ADVENTURE®

Prices and availability subject to change without notice.

- -